THE TWELVE DAYS OF TRADITION

AN AMERICAN CELEBRATION

JULIE SNOW

Copyright © 2024 by Julie Snow

All rights reserved.

No part of this book may be reproduced in any form or by any electronic or mechanical means, including information storage and retrieval systems, without written permission from the author, except for the use of brief quotations in a book review.

FOREWORD

❄

The Christmas season is a sacred time, rich with traditions that have been passed down through the generations. It is a celebration of faith, family, and the birth of our Savior, Jesus Christ. In *The 12 Days of Christmas*, I invite you on a transformative journey through this cherished tradition, blending biblical truths with a patriotic love for the values that define our great nation.

I invite you to a fresh perspective to the timeless message of Christmas, calling us to embrace the virtues of hope, love, and redemption—not just during the holiday season, but every day of our lives. With deep reverence for Scripture and a passion for preserving the foundations of our faith and freedom, she reminds us that the 12 Days of Christmas are more than a song or custom—they are a meaningful roadmap for spiritual growth and renewal.

This book becomes a guide for celebrating the birth of Christ with reverence and purpose while honoring the principles that make America a beacon of light in the world. It is an inspiring call to live boldly for truth, hold fast to our faith, and share the joy of the Gospel with a world in need.

Whether you are new to this tradition or have celebrated it for years, *The 12 Days of Christmas* will deepen your appreciation for the season and inspire you to keep its message alive in your heart and home.

May this book fill your Christmas with joy, your spirit with faith, and your heart with gratitude for the Savior who came to redeem us all.

Merry Christmas, and may God bless you and the United States of America.

THE FIRST DAY OF CHRISTMAS

On the First Day of Christmas, My True Love Gave to Me: A Partridge in a Pear Tree

. . .

Birds, pears and trees are gifts from Heaven. While we do not need to know the meaning of these gifts, let's take a look at the mysteries the Heavenly Father sent us.

Remember these are gifts not necessarily to understand but to enjoy as blessings. And to be grateful for.

As we begin the Christmas season, let's take a fresh look at the "12 Days of Christmas." with an American spirit and values that are meaningful to us as loyal Americans. The classic carol, with its memorable "partridge in a pear tree" line, holds messages that speak to us: faith, generosity, and gratitude for the gifts that surround us. Let's celebrate the "First Day of Christmas" with pride in our country, our values, and our freedoms.

Allow the American spirit to enter your soul along with the spirit of Christmas. Rejoice in knowing both are yours.

A Partridge in a Pear Tree: Faith and Sacrifice

In traditional Christian symbolism, the "partridge in a pear tree" represents Jesus Christ and his sacrifice, often described as the ultimate gift. The partridge, a bird known to protect its young, symbolizes the strength and courage of a leader who sacrifices for the good of others. For MAGA supporters, this message aligns with our own values of dedication, faith, and the appreciation of leaders who commit to serving their communities and country.

As we reflect on this first day of Christmas, let's embrace

the idea of leadership rooted in faith. Just as Christ served and sacrificed, we too can look up to leaders who uphold the values we cherish. This season, take a moment to say a prayer or hold a thought of gratitude for those in your life, or in our nation, who strive to make a positive impact—whether they're in your own family, community, or even on the national stage.

Patriotism Rooted in Faith and Tradition

For patriots, the "First Day of Christmas" offers an opportunity to appreciate the traditions that keep us grounded in what truly matters: faith, family, and freedom. The pear tree, a strong, fruitful tree, symbolizes stability and growth, much like the roots we hold in our faith and patriotic pride. Our love for this country is nourished by these values, and they are gifts we pass down to our children and communities.

Consider this: just as the pear tree stands firm and bears fruit, our devotion to faith and family creates lasting impact. Sharing these values with our loved ones—whether through Christmas traditions, prayer, or acts of service—reinforces the strength of our communities and our love for our country.

Giving Back to Honor the Gift

On this "First Day of Christmas," think of ways to give a gift back to your community that reflects the spirit of the partridge in the pear tree. Small acts of kindness, whether it's volunteering at a local church, helping a neighbor, or donating to a cause that supports veterans or first responders, can make a big difference. As MAGA supporters, showing gratitude and giving back is a part of our commitment to bettering our communities.

Let this "partridge in a pear tree" inspire you to share what you've been blessed with—be it time, resources, or simply a kind word. These acts of kindness and gratitude don't just honor the Christmas season; they honor the American spirit of giving and resilience.

This is what Christ wants!

Reflection -- A Christmas Message for All

As we go into the Twelve Days of Christmas, remember that this season is a time to cherish our faith, our freedoms, and our families. The "First Day of Christmas" with the gift of a partridge in a pear tree invites us to reflect on these values, showing us the beauty of a season that brings people together and allows us to share our blessings.

So, with a heart full of faith, let's kick off this Christmas season by celebrating the people and values that make this country great. On this first day, share a gift of gratitude, a prayer of thanks, and a commitment to uphold the blessings we hold dear as Americans. May this season remind us of all the reasons we're proud to call this country home.

THE SECOND DAY OF CHRISTMAS

On the Second Day of Christmas, My True Love Gave to Me: **Two Turtle Doves**

Strengthening Bonds Through Tradition

Another way to honor the message of the two turtle doves is by keeping traditions alive. Every family has special customs to celebrate Christmas, from the recipes passed down through generations to the unique ways we decorate our homes. This Christmas emphasize the importance of tradition in building strong family bonds. Share stories from your own family history, honor the memory of loved ones, and talk with children about what makes Christmas a time for unity and devotion.

At the same time, consider how your family traditions align with the pride and patriotism you feel as Americans. Just as we cherish personal traditions, we also respect the traditions that define our nation: freedom, faith, and community. By celebrating these values, we remind ourselves of the deep connections we share.

❄

A Message of Loyalty and Gratitude – A Reflection

On this "Second Day of Christmas," the two turtle doves call us to reflect on loyalty to faith, family, and country. Their symbolism encourages us to think about what it means to stay devoted to what we believe in and how we can bring unity and strength to our communities. Whether it's spending extra time with family, offering help to those in need, or simply remembering to be thankful for our freedoms, we can use this day to practice the true spirit of the season.

As we continue through the 12 Days of Christmas, let's carry forward the message of these two doves—a message of love, unity, and loyalty that sustains us as individuals and as a nation. May this season bring us closer to one another, inspiring us to hold fast to the values and relationships that make us proud to be Americans.

❆

THE THIRD DAY OF CHRISTMAS

On The Third Day of Christmas My True Love Gave to me: **Three French Hens**

On the third day of Christmas, the traditional carol introduces **three French hens** as a gift. These hens symbolize faith, hope, and love—three qualities that hold deep meaning during Christmas and resonate strongly with MAGA supporters who believe in the importance of holding onto core values, both in our personal lives and in our nation.

Three French Hens: Faith, Hope, and Love

Each of these "three French hens" stands for a powerful virtue:

1. **Faith**: As people of faith, we rely on our beliefs to guide us through life's ups and downs. Faith in God, family, and community strengthens us, giving us courage to face challenges with confidence. For MAGA supporters, faith also means trusting in the values that built this country and the belief that we are all here to contribute to something greater.

2. **Hope**: Hope is the light that keeps us moving forward, even in tough times. It's a belief in the possibilities of tomorrow, a sentiment that resonates deeply in the Christmas season. As patriots, we hope for a strong, united America that cherishes freedom and supports opportunity for all its citizens.

3. **Love**: Love is at the heart of Christmas—love for family, friends, and community. It's what drives us to give back, reach out, and stand together. As MAGA supporters, we also have a profound love for this country and our American way of life.

This love motivates us to work hard to preserve our freedoms and defend the values that make our country unique.

Strengthening Faith, Hope, and Love in Our Lives

The "three French hens" remind us to keep faith, hope, and love alive in our daily lives. For MAGA families, Christmas can be a time to reflect on how we can cultivate these virtues, not just during the holidays but all year long.

• **Faith** can be strengthened by prioritizing time for prayer, family, and the spiritual practices that keep us grounded. Gather with loved ones to pray or read from scripture, allowing these moments to renew your commitment to God and family.

• **Hope** can be shared by setting goals together and focusing on positive actions that support a brighter future. This could mean volunteering, getting involved in community projects, or simply encouraging family members to pursue their dreams.

• **Love** grows when we give back and support each other. Acts of kindness, whether toward family members, friends, or neighbors, create stronger communities and reinforce the bonds that unite us as Americans.

. . .

The three Hens are symbols of American resilience.

French hens, historically valued for their hardiness and ability to thrive, can also symbolize the resilience of the American spirit. As MAGA supporters, we're proud of our country's ability to face challenges, adapt, and remain strong. Just as these hens represent a reliable source of sustenance, we believe that a strong faith in American values will continue to sustain our communities and guide our future.

Take this third day of Christmas to honor the resilience you see in those around you. Maybe it's a family member who works tirelessly, a neighbor who steps up to help others, or a friend who always offers support. Acknowledge their contributions and be inspired to keep pushing forward with the same spirit.

A Commitment to Passing on Values

The gift of three French hens also reminds us of the importance of passing on our values to the next generation. Christmas is a perfect time to teach children about faith, hope, and love. Share stories from your own family history, recounting moments of resilience and faith. Show them what it means to love your country, and why these values are central to being a proud American.

Faith, Hope, and Love for Our Nation

On this third day of Christmas, we celebrate three virtues that reflect the strength of our country and the goodness of its people. Faith, hope, and love are the foundations of a resilient America. As MAGA supporters, let's embrace these values, carrying them forward not only as personal virtues but as commitments to the nation we cherish.

So, let's carry the spirit of the three French hens throughout the holiday season. May our faith in God and each other grow stronger, our hope for the future shine brighter, and our love for our country and its people deepen. As we celebrate Christmas, let us be reminded of these three gifts and the importance of cherishing and nurturing them as we work toward a bright future.

THE FOURTH DAY OF CHRISTMAS

On the Fourth Day of Christmas, My True Love Gave to Me: Four Calling Birds

On the fourth day of Christmas, the gift of **four calling birds** brings to mind messages that speak deeply to MAGA supporters: truth, courage, communication, and standing up for what we believe in. Traditionally, the "calling birds" in the carol represent voices that carry important messages—a fitting symbol for those who value the power of free speech, honest dialogue, and a commitment to staying informed.

Four Calling Birds: Voices of Truth and Freedom

Each calling bird can represent a core principle that holds meaning for this holiday season:

1. **Truth**: In today's world, seeking truth can be a challenge, but it's a cornerstone of integrity. Truth builds trust, strengthens relationships, and empowers us to make informed decisions. As MAGA supporters, standing up for truth is key, whether it's in our communities, workplaces, or within our own families. This holiday season let's take time to appreciate the power of honesty, truthfulness, and transparency in our lives.

2. **Courage**: Speaking up takes courage, especially when it challenges popular opinion. The calling birds remind us of the importance of speaking with conviction and standing firm in our beliefs. As patriots, we honor courage in all its forms—from the bravery of our military service members to those who advocate for values they hold dear. On this fourth day,

we celebrate the courage to speak our minds and support others who do the same.

3. **Communication**: Open and honest communication is essential for understanding and unity. Whether we're sharing thoughts with family, friends, or neighbors, good communication brings people together and helps us build stronger communities. This holiday season, let's focus on conversations that uplift, bridge gaps, and spread positivity. The calling birds remind us that the message we send is just as important as how we share it.

4. **Freedom**: The calling birds, in their role as messengers, remind us of the importance of protecting our freedoms—especially freedom of speech. As MAGA supporters, we understand the value of the First Amendment and the responsibility that comes with it. This freedom is what allows us to express ourselves, support our beliefs, and share ideas without fear. This Christmas let's cherish the freedoms we hold dear and stay vigilant in defending them.

Honoring Freedom of Speech and Expression

The calling birds' message on this fourth day of Christmas serves as a reminder of the importance of our voices. In a world that can sometimes feel divided, our ability to speak, share, and connect is something we can celebrate and protect. For MAGA supporters, standing up for freedom of speech is about ensuring that all voices can be heard, even those that challenge the mainstream narrative.

Consider using this holiday season to foster respectful conversations with those around you. Take time to listen, share ideas, and engage in discussions that build bridges. In doing so, we honor the calling birds' message of communication and show our commitment to a nation where freedom of thought and speech are fundamental rights.

Family Traditions and Sharing Ideas

On this fourth day of Christmas, bring the spirit of the calling birds into your family traditions. Spend time around the dinner table or the Christmas tree sharing stories, memories, and lessons that highlight the importance of truth, courage, and freedom. Encourage each family member to share something they're passionate about or grateful for, and celebrate the diversity of ideas and values within your own circle.

To deepen this tradition, you might share readings or passages that inspire these virtues. Consider including patriotic quotes, passages from the Bible, or words from American leaders that remind you of the importance of truth, courage, and unity. By nurturing these conversations, we're teaching younger generations the value of these freedoms and the responsibility that comes with them.

. . .

Supporting Voices in Your Community

Christmas is a season of giving, and one meaningful way to honor the calling birds is to support those who use their voices to serve others. This might include donating to a local charity, supporting independent journalists or organizations that uphold truth, or helping out at a community event that brings people together.

If you're looking for other ways to give back, consider writing thank-you cards to local leaders or first responders, showing appreciation for their courage and service. Simple acts of support remind us that we're all part of a larger community, and each voice—when joined with others—can make a powerful difference.

The Power of Our Collective Voice

As we continue through the 12 Days of Christmas, the calling birds remind us of the power of unity and the strength of speaking up. When we work together, share our beliefs, and listen to one another, we create a community where everyone's voice has value. The calling birds are a symbol of the collective voice of patriots who believe in America's promise and cherish the freedoms that make it unique.

On this fourth day of Christmas, let's honor the message of the calling birds by staying true to our values, speaking up with courage, and fostering conversations that strengthen our communities. May this season inspire us to use our voices for good, support one another, and continue to celebrate the freedom and unity that make this country great.

THE FIFTH DAY OF CHRISTMAS

On **The Fifth Day of Christmas My True Love Gave to Me: Five Golden Rings**

The gift of **five golden rings** on the fifth day of Christmas shines brightly as a symbol of America's treasured values and history. For MAGA supporters, five golden rings can represent the five essential pillars that make our country strong: **faith, freedom, family, prosperity, and legacy**. Each of these "rings" is part of the foundation of the American spirit and reflects qualities we seek to uphold, not just during Christmas but throughout the year.

1. Faith: A Foundation for America's Strength

- Faith has always been a cornerstone of American values, inspiring people to seek purpose, courage, and resilience. For MAGA supporters, faith isn't just a personal journey but also a shared commitment to live with integrity and serve our communities. It's a guiding principle that encourages us to pray for our families, our leaders, and our nation. Just as gold endures through time, faith remains a constant strength that unites us and gives meaning to our actions.

2. Freedom: Our Most Precious Gift

- The second golden ring symbolizes freedom, an ideal cherished by all Americans. Our freedoms—whether of speech, worship, or the right to pursue our dreams—are at the heart of our identity. Freedom requires vigilance and respect, and it's the bond that brings us together, despite our differences. This Christmas, let's remember that freedom is a gift worth fighting for, protecting, and passing down to future generations.

3. Family: The Core of Community and Nation

- Family, the third ring, is where American values take root. Strong families are essential to a strong nation, instilling respect, kindness, and perseverance. In our families, we celebrate traditions, share stories, and build legacies. This season, spending time with loved ones reminds us of the importance of family bonds and the role they play in preserving our nation's values and traditions. Family unites us, offering love, support, and guidance as we navigate life together.

4. Prosperity: The Promise of Opportunity
- The fourth ring represents prosperity, a goal we strive for through hard work, dedication, and innovation. As MAGA supporters, we believe in the American dream—the idea that everyone has the opportunity to succeed and build a better future. Prosperity allows us to support our communities, create jobs, and improve lives. This Christmas, we can reflect on our blessings and the opportunities we have to lift each other up and ensure that prosperity remains accessible to all.

5. Legacy: Honoring Our Heritage and Building the Future
- The fifth golden ring stands for legacy—the lasting impact of our actions and values. America's legacy is built by patriots who believed in freedom, justice, and equality, and today we carry forward their vision. Legacy is what we leave behind for our children and future generations, a heritage of values, ideals, and courage. This Christmas, let's commit to preserving our history, defending our principles, and working toward a future that honors our shared heritage.

Celebrating the Five Rings: A MAGA Christmas Reflection

Each of these five golden rings carries meaning that goes beyond the holidays, reminding us of the principles that bind us as Americans. To celebrate these values:

- **Take time for faith**
- **Reflect on freedom**
- **Cherish family time**
- **Appreciate prosperity**
- **Honor legacy**

On this fifth day of Christmas, may these golden rings remind us of the true gifts that define and unite us. As we celebrate faith, freedom, family, prosperity, and legacy, let's honor the American spirit and recommit ourselves to building a strong, united, and prosperous nation for generations to come.

THE SIXTH DAY OF CHRISTMAS

On The Sixth Day of Christmas, My True Love Gave to Me: Six Geese a – laying

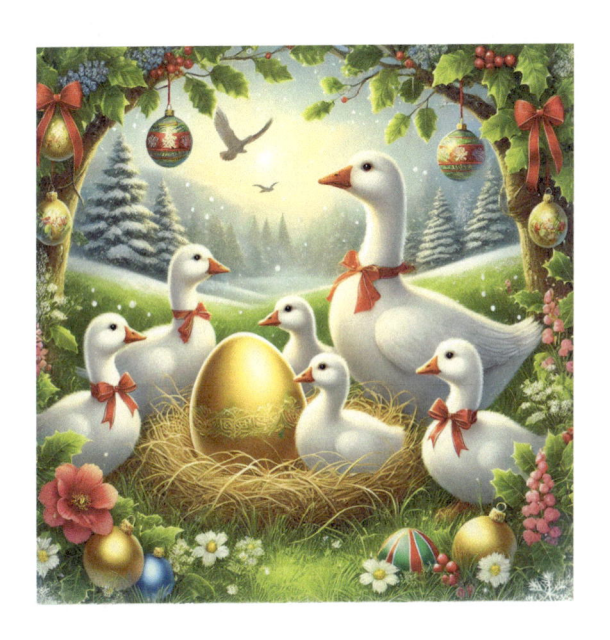

On the Sixth Day of Christmas, My True Love Gave to Me: Six Geese a-Laying

On this sixth day of Christmas, **six geese a-laying** bring a message of growth, renewal, and legacy. Just as geese lay eggs that hatch and bring new life, this gift symbolizes creation, productivity, and the blessings of abundance. For MAGA supporters, this resonates with our commitment to building a prosperous future, both for our families and our country, rooted in the values of faith, hard work, and patriotism.

Six Geese a-Laying: Nurturing Growth and Prosperity

Each of the six geese can represent an area of growth and commitment that is vital to MAGA values: **faith, family, freedom, responsibility, opportunity, and prosperity**. As they lay eggs, these geese embody the promise of new beginnings and the dedication required to protect and nurture what matters most.

1. **Faith**
2. **Family**
3. **Freedom**
4. **Responsibility**
5. **Opportunity**
6. **Prosperity**
7. **The Spirit of Hard Work and Self-Reliance**

Geese are known for their strength, teamwork, and resilience—qualities that mirror the American work ethic. For MAGA supporters, the sixth day of Christmas is a celebration of self-reliance, honoring the grit and determination that built our nation. Just as geese work together to protect and nurture their eggs, we work to support our communities, build strong families, and stand up for what we believe in.

A Christmas of Renewal and Legacy

As we embrace the symbol of the six geese, let's focus on renewal and the legacy we leave behind. This Christmas season, consider how you can nurture growth in your own life and within your family. Set goals, make plans, and encourage each other to pursue what's meaningful and true. From family traditions to personal commitments, everything we do builds toward the future we're creating.

This sixth day is a reminder that the greatest gifts aren't just things—they're the values and virtues we pass on, the communities we build, and the freedoms we protect. In this way, we lay the foundations of a stronger, more united America, honoring our heritage and creating a lasting legacy for generations to come.

So, on this day of "six geese a-laying," may we remember the blessings of growth, resilience, and dedication that make our lives and our country flourish. This Christmas, let's continue to nurture the gifts we've been given, building a future that honors our past and strengthens the foundations of America.

THE SEVENTH DAY OF CHRISTMAS

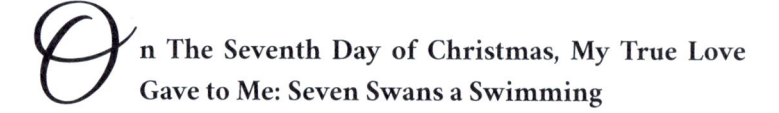

On The Seventh Day of Christmas, My True Love Gave to Me: Seven Swans a Swimming

On the Seventh Day of Christmas, My True Love Gave to Me: Seven Swans a-Swimming – A Christian Reflection

The **seven swans a-swimming** on the seventh day of Christmas hold deep symbolism in Christian tradition. In the context of the "12 Days of Christmas" carol, the seven swans often represent the **seven gifts of the Holy Spirit** as outlined in the Bible. These gifts—wisdom, understanding, counsel, fortitude, knowledge, piety, and fear of the Lord—are seen as spiritual strengths granted by God to believers, enabling them to live faithfully and serve others.

The Seven Gifts of the Holy Spirit: Seven Swans in Christian Life

Each of these gifts plays a vital role in the life of a Christian, helping us grow closer to God and embrace His calling with an open heart.

1. **Wisdom**: Wisdom allows us to see life from God's perspective, making decisions rooted in love and truth. It's a gift that brings clarity to the challenges we face and guides us to respond in ways that honor God. Like a graceful swan navigating waters, wisdom helps us navigate life with poise and understanding.

2. **Understanding**: This gift allows us to comprehend the mysteries of faith and God's word more deeply. Under-

standing brings clarity to our spiritual lives, helping us see beyond appearances and grasp the true meaning behind God's teachings.

3. **Counsel**: Counsel, or right judgment, helps us make decisions aligned with God's will. This gift allows us to listen to God's guidance in our lives and encourages us to make choices that reflect our commitment to living according to His plan.

4. **Fortitude**: Fortitude, or courage, gives us the strength to face challenges and hardships with faith and resilience. This gift enables us to stand firm in our beliefs, even in difficult situations, empowering us to live as faithful witnesses to God's love.

5. **Knowledge**: The gift of knowledge helps us understand God's purpose in the world and recognize His presence in all things. Knowledge strengthens our relationship with God and allows us to appreciate the beauty of creation, seeing His hand in every part of life.

6. **Piety**: Piety, or reverence, instills in us a deep respect for God and a desire to worship and serve Him. This gift nurtures our relationship with God as our loving Father and inspires us to live with humility, compassion, and gratitude.

. . .

7. **Fear of the Lord**: Also known as wonder and awe, this gift reminds us of God's greatness and majesty. It helps us approach Him with humility, recognizing His power and love. Fear of the Lord doesn't mean being afraid; rather, it's a reminder of God's awe-inspiring presence and our call to honor Him.

Swans: Symbols of Grace, Beauty, and Spiritual Transformation

Swans, known for their grace and beauty, symbolize spiritual transformation and purity. In Christian symbolism, a swan moving gracefully across water represents the soul's journey toward God, moving with faith and trust through the waters of life. The sight of seven swans swimming together is a beautiful reminder of unity in faith, a community bound by shared values and love for God.

Applying the Seven Gifts in Daily Life

During Christmas, a season of reflection and renewal, the seven swans a-swimming can inspire us to cultivate these gifts in our own lives. Here are a few ways to apply them:

• **Seek wisdom** by praying for God's guidance in decisions, both big and small.

• **Nurture understanding** by studying scripture or participating in Bible study, allowing God's word to deepen your faith.

• **Practice counsel** by making thoughtful choices that

honor God's teachings and seeking advice from those you trust.

• **Embrace fortitude** by facing challenges with faith, trusting that God's strength is with you in all things.

• **Grow in knowledge** by finding ways to see God's presence in everyday life, whether through nature, relationships, or quiet moments of reflection.

• **Show piety** through acts of worship, charity, and kindness, offering gratitude to God for His many blessings.

• **Honor the gift of fear of the Lord** by taking moments to appreciate God's majesty and approach Him with a heart open to awe and wonder.

A Season of Spiritual Renewal

The seven swans remind us that Christmas is not only a time of celebration but also of renewal and deepening our faith. As Christians, we're called to embrace these gifts and allow them to transform our lives, drawing us closer to God and preparing us to serve others with a joyful heart.

On this seventh day of Christmas, may the seven swans inspire us to invite the Holy Spirit into our lives. Let us reflect on these gifts and ask God to guide us in using them to bring light, hope, and love to our world. Just as swans glide gracefully across the water, may we move with grace and purpose, strengthened by the gifts God has given us.

THE EIGHTH DAY OF CHRISTMAS

On the Eighth Day of Christmas, My True Love Gave to Me: **Eight Maids a-Milking**

As we journey through the "12 Days of Christmas," the gift of **eight maids a-milking** on the eighth day symbolizes dedication, hard work, and the nurturing of our community and families. For MAGA supporters, this gift resonates deeply with values such as patriotism, support for American agriculture, family unity, and the spirit of service.

Here's how Trump supporters might embrace and celebrate the eighth day of Christmas with eight maids a-milking, honoring both tradition and the principles that strengthen our great nation.

Eight Maids a-Milking: Symbols of Hard Work and Service
In the traditional Christmas carol, the maids a-milking represent diligent work and the provision of sustenance. For MAGA supporters, this imagery aligns with the American work ethic, the importance of supporting local industries, and the commitment to ensuring that our communities thrive through collective effort.

1. **Support for American Agriculture**
    o **Celebrating Farmers and Ranchers**: The eight maids a-milking can symbolize the vital role that American farmers and ranchers play in feeding our nation and supporting the economy. Trump supporters may honor this by visiting local farms, purchasing farm-fresh products, and acknowledging the hard work that goes into sustaining our food supply.
    o **Farm-to-Table Initiatives**: Emphasizing the importance

of local produce and supporting farm-to-table movements helps strengthen the bond between consumers and producers, ensuring that American agriculture remains robust and self-sufficient.

2. **Family Unity and Traditions**

o **Gathering for a Traditional Meal**: Just as the maids provide milk, families can come together to prepare and enjoy a hearty, traditional Christmas meal. Dishes like roast turkey, homemade butter, and fresh dairy products can highlight the importance of family collaboration and the fruits of hard work.

o **Passing Down Traditions**: Engaging children in activities such as baking, cooking, or even helping with household chores reinforces the values of responsibility and teamwork. These shared moments create lasting memories and instill a sense of pride in maintaining family traditions.

3. **Community Service and Giving Back**

o **Volunteering Locally**: Emulating the service of the maids, MAGA supporters might dedicate time to volunteer at local shelters, food banks, or community centers. Providing assistance to those in need reflects the spirit of generosity and strengthens community bonds.

o **Supporting Veterans and First Responders**: Organizing or participating in events that honor veterans, police officers, and firefighters showcases gratitude for those who protect and serve our nation. Simple acts like delivering care packages or hosting appreciation dinners can make a significant impact.

4. Promoting Self-Reliance and Sustainability

o **Home Gardening and Dairy Projects**: Encouraging self-reliance, families might engage in home gardening or small-scale dairy projects, such as keeping a few chickens for fresh eggs or maintaining a vegetable garden. These activities promote sustainability and the value of producing one's own food.

o **DIY Projects and Crafts**: Creating handmade items, whether it's crafting decorative milk bottles or building simple farm-inspired decorations, fosters creativity and the satisfaction of building something with one's own hands.

5. Patriotic Celebrations and Decorations

o **Patriotic-Themed Decor**: Incorporating red, white, and blue elements into Christmas decorations can blend the symbolism of the maids a-milking with patriotic pride. American flags, star-shaped ornaments, and farm-themed decorations can create a festive atmosphere that honors both tradition and country.

o **Celebrating American Heritage**: Sharing stories of American pioneers, farmers, and community leaders during holiday gatherings reinforces the importance of heritage and the contributions of those who built and sustain our nation.

Embracing the Spirit of the Eight Maids a-Milking

The eighth day of Christmas with eight maids a-milking is a celebration of the values that MAGA supporters hold dear: hard work, family unity, community service, and patriotic pride. By embracing these principles, we honor not only the spirit of Christmas but also the enduring strength and resilience of the American people.

Practical Ways to Celebrate

- **Host a Community Potluck**: Invite neighbors and friends to share dishes made from local ingredients, fostering a sense of community and mutual support.
- **Create a Gratitude List**: Encourage each family member to list things they are thankful for, emphasizing the blessings of hard work, family, and freedom.
- **Organize a Charity Drive**: Collect donations for a local charity, such as a food bank or veterans' organization, and involve the whole family in the effort to give back.
- **Decorate Together**: Spend an evening decorating the home with farm-inspired and patriotic ornaments, making it a fun and collaborative family activity.
- **Share Stories of Hard Work and Perseverance**: During Christmas gatherings, share stories that highlight the importance of dedication and resilience, whether from personal experiences or historical figures.

A Christmas of Dedication and Gratitude

As MAGA supporters celebrate the eighth day of Christmas with eight maids a-milking, the focus is on honoring the values of hard work, service, and family unity. This celebration is a testament to the enduring American spirit, where each effort, no matter how small, contributes to the greater good of our nation. By embracing these traditions, we not only enrich our own lives but also strengthen the communities that make America the land of opportunity and prosperity.

May this Christmas season inspire us to continue working diligently, serving our communities with pride, and cherishing the blessings of family and freedom. As we honor the eight maids a-milking, let us celebrate the heart and soul of America, ensuring that our traditions and values are passed down to future generations with love and dedication.

THE NINTH DAY OF CHRISTMAS

On the Ninth Day of Christmas, My True Love Gave to Me: Nine Ladies Dancing

As the Christmas season continues through the Twelve Days, the ninth day brings with it a unique significance. Traditionally, the "Ninth Day of Christmas" refers to the "nine ladies dancing," as mentioned in the beloved carol, "The Twelve Days of Christmas." For Christians, this day serves as an opportunity to reflect on the deeper meanings within the symbolism of "nine," and to focus on the Fruit of the Spirit.

Exploring the Symbolism of the Ninth Day

The concept of "nine ladies dancing" may seem whimsical at first, but this image holds significant meaning. In Christian tradition, dancing can represent joy and freedom in the presence of God, which aligns with the joy of salvation celebrated in the Christmas season. Dancing here reflects the overflowing happiness that comes from knowing Christ, with the "nine ladies" symbolizing the nine qualities of the Fruit of the Spirit: love, joy, peace, patience, kindness, goodness, faithfulness, gentleness, and self-control.

These qualities represent the character of a life transformed by God's grace and are meant to be evident in the lives of believers. The ninth day, then, is a call to focus on how we embody these virtues in our daily walk with Christ and how we can let the Spirit shape us more fully.

The Fruit of the Spirit: A Deeper Reflection

The Fruit of the Spirit, described in Paul's letter to the Galatians, is a set of virtues that grows in a Christian's life as they draw closer to God. Each fruit represents an aspect of Christ's character and, collectively, reflects a life surrendered to God's guidance. Reflecting on each fruit on this ninth day offers Christians a framework to assess their spiritual journey.

1. **Love**: This foundational fruit permeates all others. Christian love is sacrificial, patient, and unselfish. It seeks the good of others, just as Christ demonstrated through His life and sacrifice.

2. **Joy**: Different from mere happiness, joy is a deep and abiding gladness rooted in God's promises. Despite life's trials, joy remains because it depends on God's unchanging nature rather than external circumstances.

3. **Peace**: The peace of Christ surpasses all understanding, giving us tranquility in the midst of chaos. This peace is not only an inner calm but also leads us to become peacemakers in our relationships and communities.

4. **Patience**: Often described as long-suffering, patience is the strength to endure hardships and delay without becoming angry or disillusioned. It reflects the patience God shows us in His grace and mercy.

5. **Kindness**: Reflecting God's kindness toward us, this fruit leads us to acts of compassion and empathy. Kindness sees

beyond faults and seeks to offer gentleness and support to those in need.

6. **Goodness**: Goodness involves a commitment to moral integrity and righteousness. It is a call to stand firm in God's truth and pursue holiness.

7. **Faithfulness**: Faithfulness speaks to loyalty and reliability. It reminds us to remain steadfast in our faith, keeping our commitments to God and to others.

8. **Gentleness**: Gentleness is a quality of humility, strength under control. It calls us to approach others with respect and compassion, recognizing our shared humanity.

9. **Self-Control**: This final fruit is the ability to resist temptation and practice discipline. Through self-control, we keep our actions, thoughts, and words in line with God's will.

Living Out the Ninth Day

The Christmas season, while joyful, can often highlight our struggles to live out these virtues fully. For some, it's a time of family gatherings that can test patience and self-control. For others, it may be a season marked by loss or loneliness, challenging their joy and peace. The ninth day serves as a reminder that the Fruit of the Spirit grows not by our own efforts but through our reliance on God's presence within us.

Prayer and Reflection on the Ninth Day

On this day, Christians can take time to pray and reflect on how they are cultivating the Fruit of the Spirit. Here are a few practical ways to do this:

1. **Journaling**: Write down each of the nine fruits and consider where you see these qualities in your life. Which are strongest? Which could use growth? This exercise offers an honest assessment and an opportunity for growth.

2. **Scripture Reading**: Studying passages about each fruit deepens understanding and gives insight into living them out. For example, 1 Corinthians 13 provides a beautiful portrait of love, while Philippians 4:4-7 speaks to joy and peace in Christ.

3. **Pray for Growth**: Ask the Holy Spirit to help you grow in

specific areas. Surrendering each fruit to God's care is a powerful step in allowing the Spirit to transform you.

Celebrating with the Christian Community

The Christian journey is meant to be shared, and the ninth day is an ideal time to celebrate within the community. Hosting a small gathering or even a virtual celebration focused on gratitude for the ways God is at work in each person's life can be a meaningful way to honor this day. Each person might share about one of the fruits they've seen developing in their life, or perhaps offer a word of encouragement to others in the group.

Remembering the Call to Faithfulness

Faithfulness, one of the nine fruits, is particularly relevant on the ninth day. Christmas is, after all, a story of faithfulness: God's faithfulness to His promise of a Savior, Mary and Joseph's faithfulness to their calling, and the faith of the shepherds and wise men who followed God's guidance to find Christ. As Christians, we are called to emulate that faithfulness—not just in this season but in every season of life.

Faithfulness Works as a Foundation for New Beginnings

The ninth day of Christmas often falls close to the New Year, a natural time for reflection and resolutions. For Christians, this day provides a reminder that our goals and aspirations should align with the character of Christ. As you set intentions for the coming year, let the Fruit of the Spirit serve as a guide for what to pursue.

A Prayer for the Ninth Day

Here is a prayer that can be used to mark this day:

"Heavenly Father, we thank You for the gift of Your Spirit, who works within us to bear fruit that reflects Your love. On this ninth day of Christmas, we ask that You strengthen each of these fruits in our lives. Let our love be genuine, our joy steadfast, and our peace unshakeable. Teach us patience and kindness, guide us in goodness, help us to remain faithful, and fill us with gentleness and self-control. May we grow in these qualities each day as we draw nearer to You. In Jesus' name, we pray. Amen."

Conclusion: Embracing the Spirit of Christmas Year-Round

The ninth day of Christmas reminds us that the true gift of the season is not just for twelve days but for a lifetime. The Fruit of the Spirit is a daily reminder of how Christ's birth continues to shape us. As we carry these lessons forward, let the joy and gratitude of Christmas inspire us to live out each day with love, peace, and faithfulness, bringing light to the world as Christ has brought light to us.

THE TENTH DAY OF CHRISTMAS

On the Tenth Day of Christmas, My True Love Gave to Me:
Ten Lords A-Leaping

The Tenth Day of Christmas: Embracing the Ten Commandments and Living a Life of Obedience

In Christian tradition, the Twelve Days of Christmas are celebrated not only as a festive period but also as an extended time for reflection on spiritual themes and biblical teachings. Each day has symbolic meaning, and the "Tenth Day of Christmas" is often associated with the Ten Commandments. This day provides an opportunity to reflect on the commandments given by God as a guide for righteous living and a foundation for building a faithful community.

As we continue in the Christmas season, the tenth day invites Christians to contemplate the significance of the Ten Commandments, considering how these ancient principles remain relevant in modern life. More than a set of rules, they represent God's desire for His people to live in harmony with Him and each other, embodying a life of obedience and holiness.

The Symbolism of the Tenth Day

The Ten Commandments, given by God to Moses on Mount Sinai, are central to both Jewish and Christian teachings. In the context of Christmas, they remind us that Jesus came to fulfill God's law and to show us how to live in accordance with God's will. The commandments cover both our relationship with God and our relationships with one another, reflecting a moral standard that has been foundational in the Judeo-Christian tradition for centuries.

On this tenth day, Christians are encouraged to reflect on these commandments, not as a checklist of requirements but as a blueprint for a faithful, fulfilling, and God-centered life.

Revisiting the Ten Commandments

Let's briefly explore each commandment and consider how it applies to the lives of Christians today.

1. **"You shall have no other gods before Me."**

This commandment calls for exclusive devotion to God. In a world filled with distractions and competing priorities, this first commandment reminds Christians to keep God at the center of their lives. It encourages believers to examine the "gods" or idols they might be tempted to prioritize, whether they be wealth, success, or other pursuits, and to realign their focus on God.

2. **"You shall not make for yourself an image..."**

This commandment warns against creating idols. It is a call to worship God as He truly is, rather than creating our own interpretations or versions of Him. In today's context, it is a reminder not to reduce God to our preferences or misunderstandings, but to approach Him with reverence and awe.

3. **"You shall not take the name of the Lord your God in vain."**

Respect for God's name speaks to the importance of revering Him not just in words but in our actions and character. Taking God's name seriously means living in a way that honors Him, both in speech and in the way we represent Him to others.

4. **"Remember the Sabbath day, to keep it holy."**

The Sabbath is a day of rest and worship. In today's fast-paced world, this commandment invites Christians to find regular time for rest and spiritual rejuvenation. It serves as a reminder to set aside distractions, connect with God, and recharge spiritually.

5. **"Honor your father and your mother."**

This commandment highlights the importance of family and respect for one's elders. Beyond literal parents, it encourages respect for all authorities God has placed in our lives and reminds us of the value of family unity and intergenerational respect.

6. **"You shall not murder."**

The sixth commandment speaks to the sanctity of life, reminding us to value and protect others. Jesus expanded on this commandment by teaching that even anger toward others is harmful. It calls us to foster peace, compassion, and a deep respect for human dignity.

7. "**You shall not commit adultery.**"

This commandment protects the sanctity of marriage and relationships. It urges Christians to honor commitments and remain faithful, as well as to respect the boundaries in relationships, whether romantic or otherwise.

8. "**You shall not steal.**"

More than avoiding theft, this commandment challenges us to respect others' rights, property, and work. It encourages generosity and fairness and reminds us of the value of integrity in our dealings with others.

9. "**You shall not bear false witness against your neighbor.**"

Truthfulness is essential to building trust within a community. This commandment warns against lying and slander, encouraging us to speak truthfully and justly and to avoid gossip that could harm others.

10. "**You shall not covet...**"

Coveting, or desiring what others have, leads to envy and discontent. This commandment calls us to practice contentment and gratitude, recognizing the blessings we have and trusting God to meet our needs.

. . .

Reflecting on the Commandments as a Framework for Christian Living

On the tenth day of Christmas, reflecting on the Ten Commandments provides a powerful foundation for the coming year. In the same way that Jesus fulfilled the law through His life and teachings, Christians are called to live in a way that honors these principles, both outwardly and inwardly.

Jesus and the Commandments

When Jesus was asked about the greatest commandment, He summarized the law with two overarching principles: "Love the Lord your God with all your heart and with all your soul and with all your mind" and "Love your neighbor as yourself" (Matthew 22:37-39). In these words, He captured the essence of the Ten Commandments—the first four relating to our relationship with God and the latter six relating to our relationship with others.

As Christians celebrate Christmas and the coming of Christ, the tenth day offers a moment to commit to living out these commandments, grounded in the love that Jesus demonstrated.

Obedience and Freedom in Christ

Some people may view commandments as restrictive rules, but within the Christian faith, obedience to God's commands is seen as a path to true freedom. Jesus Himself said, "If you love me, keep my commands" (John 14:15). Obeying God is not about legalistic rule-keeping but about cultivating a loving, respectful relationship with Him. Obedience allows us to live in the fullness of God's grace, experiencing the joy and peace that comes from following His guidance.

A Prayer for the Tenth Day of Christmas

Here is a prayer that Christians can reflect on during this day:

"Lord, on this tenth day of Christmas, we thank You for the gift of Your commandments. They are a lamp to our feet and a guide to our path. Help us to embrace Your wisdom and live in a way that reflects Your love. Teach us to love You with all our hearts, and to love others as ourselves. May we live out these principles each day as a testimony to Your goodness. In Jesus' name, we pray. Amen."

Living Out the Tenth Day

On this day, consider setting time aside for meditation and prayer, focusing on the Ten Commandments. Reflect on how each commandment applies to different areas of your life. You might choose to journal about areas where you need God's help to follow His guidance, or ways in which you can more fully embody the love of Christ in your relationships.

. . .

Conclusion: The Tenth Day of Christmas as a Call to Faithfulness

The tenth day of Christmas serves as a reminder that the Christmas season is about more than celebration; it's also about transformation. As we reflect on the Ten Commandments, we see not only the standard of God's holiness but also a path toward deeper faithfulness and freedom in Christ. By allowing the spirit of the commandments to shape our lives, we honor the gift of Jesus and celebrate Christmas in its fullest, truest sense.

Through commitment, prayer, and reflection, Christians can take the lessons of this day forward into the coming year, letting God's wisdom guide them toward a life marked by love, peace, and righteousness.

In the traditional Christmas carol, "The Twelve Days of Christmas," each day symbolizes something deeper within Christian teachings, and "ten lords a-leaping" on the tenth day holds particular significance. Christian interpretations often see this image as symbolizing the **Ten Commandments**, given by God to Moses on Mount Sinai. This connection brings out themes of obedience, moral authority, and a commitment to live righteously according to God's guidelines.

Here's a breakdown of how "ten lords a-leaping" connects to Christian symbolism and teaching:

. . .

1. Lords Represent Authority and Law
- In the context of the carol, lords are seen as figures of authority, akin to leaders or judges who uphold law and order. The Ten Commandments, as divine laws given by God, represent the ultimate moral authority. Just as earthly lords in historical contexts would issue decrees and expect obedience, the Ten Commandments call for respect and adherence.

2. Leaping as a Symbol of Joyful Obedience
- The image of lords "leaping" suggests joyful, enthusiastic movement, which can be interpreted as a response of gladness to God's law. Rather than viewing the Ten Commandments as mere restrictions, this image highlights that God's law brings freedom, joy, and purpose. In the Christian understanding, obedience to God's commands leads not to confinement but to a fulfilling, liberated life.
- Psalm 19:8 says, "The precepts of the Lord are right, giving joy to the heart," reinforcing the idea that following God's ways can bring joy.

3. The Ten Commandments as Foundations of Christian Living
- The Ten Commandments are foundational to both Jewish and Christian morality. Each commandment teaches us how to honor God and respect one another. The first four commandments focus on our relationship with God (e.g., no other gods, keeping the Sabbath), while the remaining six outline principles for relating to others (e.g., honoring parents, not stealing, not coveting).

- By associating the tenth day with "ten lords a-leaping," Christians reflect on these commandments as timeless principles that still apply in today's world, guiding believers in their faith journey and daily interactions.

4. Celebrating the Commandments as Part of Christmas

- Associating the Ten Commandments with the tenth day of Christmas helps tie the celebration of Jesus' birth to a commitment to live according to God's standards. Jesus himself emphasized the importance of these commandments in the New Testament, saying that the essence of the law is to love God with all one's heart and to love one's neighbor as oneself (Matthew 22:37-40).
- Reflecting on the Ten Commandments at Christmas encourages believers to honor the season by examining how well they embody these principles of love, honesty, and respect in their lives.

5. Obedience as an Act of Worship

- Obeying the Ten Commandments, as represented by the lords, can be seen as a way of honoring God. Christians believe that true worship extends beyond songs and prayers; it includes living a life that aligns with God's will. The image of lords dancing joyfully underscores the idea that obeying God's law is a way to celebrate Him, bringing joy both to God and to the believer.

Christian Reflection on the "Ten Lords a-Leaping"

For Christians, reflecting on the "ten lords a-leaping" serves as an invitation to evaluate one's own commitment to living in alignment with the Ten Commandments. As people celebrate the Christmas season, it becomes a call to deepen one's faith by striving to embody the love, respect, and integrity that the commandments encourage. Each commandment speaks to a facet of righteous living:

• **Commitment to God** (first four commandments): How can one draw closer to God and make Him the center of life?

• **Respect for Others** (last six commandments): How does one's behavior reflect love and fairness toward family, neighbors, and even strangers?

The "ten lords a-leaping" on the tenth day of Christmas can thus be seen as a vibrant symbol of joyfully committing to God's way and celebrating a life that aligns with His teachings.

THE ELEVENTH DAY OF CHRISTMAS

On the Eleventh Day of Christmas: My True Love Gave to Me Eleven Pipers Pipin'

The Eleventh Day of Christmas: Embracing the Faith of the Eleven Faithful Apostles

In Christian tradition, each day in the "Twelve Days of Christmas" holds unique symbolic significance, with the eleventh day representing the "eleven faithful apostles." The concept of "eleven pipers piping" from the carol, "The Twelve Days of Christmas," can be interpreted in Christian teachings as a celebration of the eleven apostles who remained faithful to Jesus, even after His betrayal by Judas Iscariot. Reflecting on these eleven apostles on the eleventh day of Christmas provides Christians an opportunity to delve into themes of faithfulness, discipleship, and the Great Commission.

The Eleven Faithful Apostles: Symbols of Commitment and Perseverance

The apostles—originally twelve—were the closest disciples of Jesus, chosen specifically to witness His ministry, teachings, miracles, and ultimately, His death and resurrection. However, one of them, Judas Iscariot, betrayed Jesus, leaving eleven who stayed loyal and took up His call to spread the gospel. Each of these apostles, in his own way, provides a model of courage, dedication, and the willingness to endure hardships in service to Christ.

The eleven faithful apostles include:
1. **Peter**
2. **Andrew**
3. **James (son of Zebedee)**
4. **John**
5. **Philip**
6. **Bartholomew**

7. **Thomas**
8. **Matthew**
9. **James (son of Alphaeus)**
10. **Thaddaeus (also known as Jude)**
11. **Simon the Zealot**

Each of these men answered the call to follow Jesus, spreading the message of hope, forgiveness, and redemption after His ascension. Their lives and sacrifices are remembered as examples of unwavering faith and commitment to the mission of Christ.

Faithfulness in the Face of Adversity

One of the primary themes of the eleventh day is faithfulness. The eleven apostles, though flawed and human, ultimately stayed faithful to Jesus, even when it required immense personal sacrifice. After Jesus' death and resurrection, they faced intense persecution, often risking their lives to continue sharing the gospel. Their faithfulness was not without struggles or doubts, as many of them grappled with fear and uncertainty, especially during the initial days after Jesus' crucifixion.

Yet, empowered by the Holy Spirit at Pentecost, they became bold witnesses to the truth they had seen. This transformation reminds Christians that faithfulness to Christ can be a journey of growth, courage, and surrender. Just as the apostles had to overcome personal doubts and external opposition, Christians today are called to remain faithful, even when it requires courage or sacrifice.

The Great Commission: A Call to Spread the Gospel

In the days following Jesus' resurrection, He appeared to the eleven faithful apostles and issued the Great Commission, instructing them to "go and make disciples of all nations, baptizing them in the name of the Father and of the Son and of the Holy Spirit" (Matthew 28:19). This commission has become the cornerstone of Christian missionary work and evangelism. On the eleventh day of Christmas, Christians reflect on this commission, recognizing the apostles' role in bringing the gospel to the world and understanding their own part in continuing this mission today.

The eleven apostles became the foundation of the early Church, establishing Christian communities throughout the known world, from Jerusalem to far-reaching regions. Their commitment to Jesus' command is a powerful reminder that each believer has a role in sharing the message of Christ. Whether through words, actions, or lifestyles, Christians are called to live in a way that reflects the love and teachings of Jesus.

Lessons from the Lives of the Eleven Apostles

Each apostle's life offers distinct lessons and insights that remain relevant to Christians today. Reflecting on their individual journeys on the eleventh day of Christmas can inspire believers in their own walk of faith:

1. **Peter** – Despite his impulsive nature and denial of Jesus, Peter emerged as a central leader in the early Church. His life shows that God can use even the flawed and repentant to accomplish great things.

2. **Andrew** – Known for introducing people to Jesus, Andrew reminds Christians of the importance of inviting others to experience the love of Christ.

3. **James (son of Zebedee)** – James was among the first to be martyred, illustrating the call to courageously stand for one's faith, even at great personal cost.

4. **John** – Often called "the beloved disciple," John's writings emphasize the importance of love, urging Christians to embody love as central to their faith.

5. **Philip** – Known for his thoughtful questions and evangelism, Philip inspires believers to seek understanding and clarity in faith while sharing it boldly.

6. **Bartholomew (also known as Nathanael)** – A man of integrity, Bartholomew's story emphasizes the value of sincerity and authenticity in one's relationship with Christ.

7. **Thomas** – Often remembered as "Doubting Thomas," his eventual belief after doubt shows that faith can emerge stronger through honest questioning.

8. **Matthew** – Once a tax collector, Matthew's life is a powerful testament to Jesus' ability to transform lives and use unlikely individuals for His purposes.

9. **James (son of Alphaeus)** – Though lesser-known, James

teaches the value of humble service, showing that God's work doesn't always require prominence.

10. **Thaddaeus (Jude)** – Thaddaeus reminds believers of the call to serve faithfully without seeking recognition.

11. **Simon the Zealot** – His background as a Zealot shows that Jesus unites people from all walks of life and calls them to a higher purpose beyond political or social affiliations.

Reflecting on each of these apostles encourages Christians to consider how their own unique gifts, personalities, and backgrounds can be used in the service of Christ's kingdom.

Faithful Discipleship: Following in the Apostles' Footsteps

The eleventh day of Christmas provides an opportunity for Christians to reflect on what it means to be a true disciple. Just as the eleven apostles were called to follow Jesus and spread His teachings, each believer is called to a life of discipleship. This requires:

• **Commitment**: Like the apostles, believers are called to stay committed to Christ, even when facing trials.

• **Obedience**: The apostles demonstrated obedience by leaving behind their old lives to follow Jesus. Modern Christians, too, are called to follow Christ's teachings, even when they conflict with societal trends.

• **Dependence on the Holy Spirit**: Just as the apostles received the Holy Spirit at Pentecost, Christians today are encouraged to rely on the Holy Spirit for strength, guidance, and courage in living out their faith.

A Prayer for the Eleventh Day

"Heavenly Father, on this eleventh day of Christmas, we thank You for the eleven faithful apostles who dedicated their lives to Your work. Help us to embrace their faithfulness, courage, and dedication as we strive to live as true disciples of Christ. May we be bold in sharing Your love and faithful in our commitment to follow You, no matter the cost. Empower us with Your Spirit to carry forth the mission You have entrusted to us. In Jesus' name, we pray. Amen."

Conclusion: Celebrating the Legacy of Faith

The eleventh day of Christmas serves as a reminder of the legacy of the apostles who laid the foundation for the Church and faithfully spread the gospel. Christians today inherit this legacy, called to continue sharing the message of Christ with the same commitment, courage, and love. Reflecting on the lives and sacrifices of the eleven faithful apostles encourages believers to deepen their discipleship, trust God's guidance, and embrace their part in His mission.

As the Christmas season nears its close, the eleventh day stands as an enduring call to faithfulness and dedication, inspiring Christians to live each day with the same passion and purpose as the apostles. Through their example, Christians are reminded that faith, when lived out with courage and love, can transform lives and bring light to the world, just as it did through the lives of the eleven faithful apostles.

THE TWELFTH DAY OF CHRISTMAS

On the Twelfth Day of Christmas: My True Love Gave to Me 12 Drummers Drummin'

The Twelfth Day of Christmas: Celebrating the Twelve Points of the Apostles' Creed

In Christian tradition, the twelfth day of Christmas, often celebrated as Epiphany Eve or "Twelfth Night," brings the Twelve Days of Christmas to a close. This day, symbolized in the carol by "twelve drummers drumming," is commonly interpreted as a celebration of the **twelve points of the Apostles' Creed**. In this context, the drumming represents the strength, unity, and conviction of these essential beliefs that form the foundation of Christian faith.

The Apostles' Creed is one of the oldest and most universally accepted Christian creeds, summarizing core Christian doctrines about God, Jesus Christ, the Holy Spirit, and the Church. Reflecting on the twelve points of this creed on the twelfth day serves as a reaffirmation of faith and commitment to Christian teachings.

The Twelve Drummers Drumming: A Symbol of Conviction and Faith

The image of "twelve drummers drumming" carries a few key symbolic meanings in Christian interpretation:

1. **Strength and Steadfastness**: Drums have traditionally symbolized strength, consistency, and endurance. The steady beat of the drum can be seen as a metaphor for the enduring and unwavering nature of Christian faith. Just as a drumbeat maintains rhythm and unifies, so do the beliefs outlined in the Apostles' Creed hold believers together in a shared faith.

2. **Proclamation of Belief**: Drummers often announce and

proclaim, echoing a sense of declaration. The twelve points of the Apostles' Creed summarize the fundamental beliefs of Christianity. Drumming can symbolize the bold proclamation of these truths, encouraging Christians to confidently declare their faith to the world.

3. **Unity and Community**: Drumming brings people together, symbolizing unity. The creed serves as a common foundation for Christians across denominations and traditions, reminding them of their shared beliefs and identity in Christ. It binds the Christian community, just as a shared rhythm unites those who march or dance to it.

The Twelve Points of the Apostles' Creed

The Apostles' Creed is traditionally divided into twelve points of faith. Each point corresponds to a belief that Christians hold about God, Jesus, and the work of the Holy Spirit. On the twelfth day, Christians are invited to reflect on each of these truths as they conclude the Christmas season:

1. "**I believe in God, the Father Almighty, Maker of heaven and earth.**"

o This affirms belief in God as the Creator of all things and the sovereign Lord over creation. It underscores God's power, authority, and love as a father to His people.

2. "**And in Jesus Christ, His only Son, our Lord.**"

o This point highlights the belief in Jesus as God's only Son and the Lord of all. Recognizing Jesus' divine identity is central to Christian faith.

3. "**Who was conceived by the Holy Spirit, born of the Virgin Mary.**"

o This emphasizes the miraculous and divine nature of Jesus' birth, affirming both His divinity and humanity. It also affirms the role of the Holy Spirit and Mary in God's plan of salvation.

4. **"He suffered under Pontius Pilate, was crucified, died, and was buried."**

o This reminds Christians of the reality of Jesus' suffering and death, underscoring the sacrifice He made for humanity's salvation.

5. **"He descended into hell."**

o Traditionally interpreted as Jesus' victory over death and sin, this point affirms that Jesus overcame the powers of darkness and separation from God.

6. **"The third day He rose again from the dead."**

o This celebrates Jesus' resurrection, the central event of Christian faith, which provides hope for eternal life and triumph over death.

7. **"He ascended into heaven and is seated at the right hand of God the Father Almighty."**

o This proclaims Jesus' exaltation and ongoing role as an intercessor for humanity, reigning with God the Father in heaven.

8. **"From there He shall come to judge the living and the dead."**

o This looks forward to the Second Coming of Christ and the final judgment, affirming that Jesus will return to bring justice and establish His kingdom fully.

9. **"I believe in the Holy Spirit."**

o This declares belief in the Holy Spirit, who empowers, guides, and comforts believers, continuing God's work on earth through the Church.

10. "**The holy catholic Church, the communion of saints.**"

o "Catholic" here refers to the universal Church, transcending denominational lines. This point emphasizes the unity and fellowship of believers across all times and places.

11. "**The forgiveness of sins.**"

o This celebrates God's mercy and grace in forgiving sins, made possible through Jesus' sacrifice, and is central to Christian teachings on redemption.

12. "**The resurrection of the body, and life everlasting.**"

o This final point affirms the hope of eternal life and the resurrection, a promise that gives Christians purpose, hope, and peace.

Reflecting on the Creed as a Framework for Faith

The twelve points of the Apostles' Creed represent the core beliefs that unite Christians. On the twelfth day of Christmas, Christians are encouraged to reflect on each of these truths, considering their significance in personal faith. Reciting the creed or contemplating its meaning can serve as a recommitment to these foundational beliefs.

The creed's affirmation of God's love, Jesus' redemptive work, and the ongoing presence of the Holy Spirit encourages Christians to deepen their understanding of these core doctrines and allows them to feel connected to the broader Christian community, past and present.

Living Out the Twelfth Day of Christmas

As the Christmas season concludes, the twelfth day is a

time for Christians to recommit to living according to these beliefs. Each point of the Apostles' Creed calls Christians not only to affirm their faith but to live it actively. Here are a few ways to live out the spirit of the twelfth day:

1. **Reaffirm Your Faith**: Take time to pray, recite, or meditate on the Apostles' Creed, allowing it to remind you of the truths you hold dear.

2. **Engage with Christian Community**: As the creed emphasizes unity, spend time with other believers, whether in a service, small group, or personal gathering, to reflect on what the creed means in community.

3. **Commit to Sharing the Faith**: Just as the twelve drummers represent the bold proclamation of belief, consider how you might share the message of Jesus with others, letting your life reflect the hope and truth of the creed.

4. **Embrace the Hope of Resurrection and Eternal Life**: The twelfth point offers a promise of eternal life, which brings hope beyond life's challenges. Allow this hope to bring you peace and encourage you to live purposefully each day.

A Prayer for the Twelfth Day

"Lord, on this twelfth day of Christmas, we thank You for the gift of faith and the truths revealed in the Apostles' Creed. Strengthen our belief in You and help us to live in a way that reflects these core values. As we end this season, may our faith be renewed, our hearts encouraged, and our spirits emboldened to proclaim Your truth. Guide us, empower us, and keep us faithful in our journey with You. In Jesus' name, we pray. Amen."

Conclusion: Embracing the Faith We Proclaim

The twelfth day of Christmas brings the season to a close by calling Christians to reflect on the beliefs that define their faith. The "twelve drummers drumming" symbolize the rhythm of conviction that should characterize a Christian's life, echoing the steady beat of unwavering faith. As believers celebrate the twelfth day, they are reminded to live out these values each day, grounded in the creed's truths and inspired by the hope of the gospel.

The Twelfth Day of Christmas is not just an ending but a beginning—a call to carry the joy, faith, and commitment of the Christmas season forward, empowered to live each day in the light of Christ's truth.

BLESS YOU!

*A*s we conclude *"The 12 Days Tradition/ An American Celebration"*, we want to thank you for joining us on this journey of faith, patriotism, and celebration. Your commitment to keeping Christ at the center of this season and standing together as a community of believers is a powerful testimony to the strength of our faith and fellowship.

May your heart be filled with joy, your home with peace, and your future with hope as we continue to walk in faith and freedom together. This Christmas, let us cherish the bonds of family, friendship, and shared purpose, remembering the ultimate gift of love that Christ gave to us all.

From our hearts to yours, we wish you a very Merry Christmas and a blessed New Year. Together, let us shine His light, strengthen our faith, and build a brighter tomorrow for His glory.

God bless you, and God bless America.

Sincerely,

Julie Snow

Made in the USA
Columbia, SC
09 December 2024